KID FORCE 3

GENERAL MAYHEM

TONY BRADMAN   JAKE HILL

EDGE FRANKLIN WATTS

LONDON·SYDNEY

Franklin Watts
First published in Great Britain in 2019 by The Watts Publishing Group

Executive Editor: Adrian Cole
Project Editor: Katie Woolley
Designer: Cathryn Gilbert
Illustrations: Jake Hill

HB ISBN 978 1 4451 5632 3
PB ISBN 978 1 4451 5633 0
Library ebook ISBN 978 1 4451 6361 1

Printed in China

Franklin Watts
An imprint of
Hachette Children's Group
Part of The Watts Publishing Group
Carmelite House
50 Victoria Embankment
London EC4Y 0DZ

An Hachette UK Company
www.hachette.co.uk

www.franklinwatts.co.uk

Layla   Jayden   Caleb

They are…

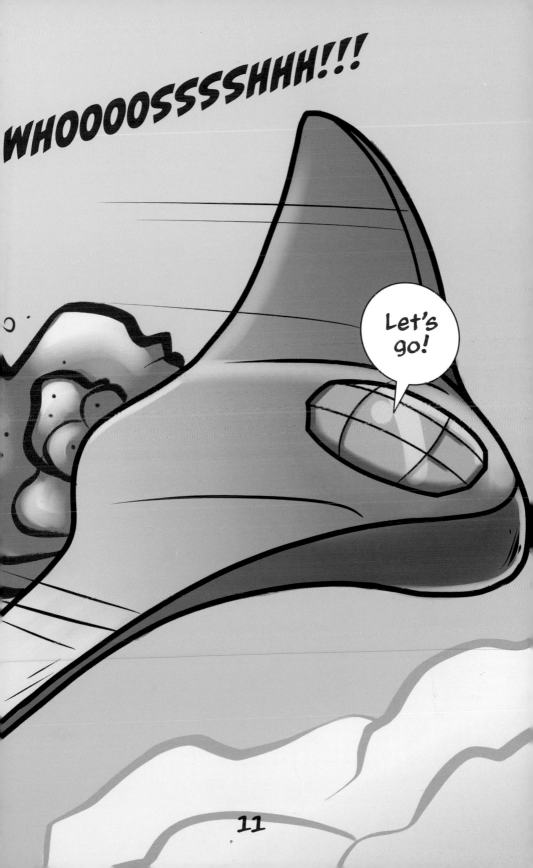

"I kidnapped your friend so you would come," said General Mayhem. "I have an offer for you. With my brains and your super powers, we can take over the world!"

29